HeLLfIRe

A MIDNIGHT EYE FILE

William Meikle

CONTENTS

I

L et me tell you about the time I went into Joe's shop for a packet of fags and came out with one of my strangest cases.

It was a warm Saturday in July. The hallway that doubled as my office was too hot, I hadn't had a whisper of a client for a week and I was tired of my own company. I put on my thinnest suit jacket, didn't bother with a tie and headed out for a beer.

First stop was Joe's place where the plan was to replenish the smokes before heading for the Twa Dugs and some shady pleasures. Joe was where he always is, shuffling from one foot to the other behind the counter where he'd stood for the past twenty-odd years I'd known him and God alone knows for how long before that.

"Ah, Derek," he said, looking up when the bell chimed above the door, "we were just talking about you."

An elderly lady I didn't recognize stood opposite Joe at the counter. Her eyes looked red and wet from crying and I immediately wished I'd headed straight for the pub; I don't do well with weeping older women, they tend to revert me to a much younger man, a grandson willing to do anything to please. I told myself as I walked forward that this time it wouldn't work, this time I wouldn't be an easy touch.

My resolve lasted only as long as it took her to reach out and take my hand.

WILLIAM MEIKLE

"A big lad like you is just what I need," she said, and I feared the worst; there's a certain brand of auld women in these parts that take great delight in chasing younger men, mainly for the amount of pure red-faced embarrassment they can cause. But it turned out she wasn't one of those; her tears when she clasped my hand as if it was a small dog were real enough.

"She had on her green duffel coat. That should mean she's easy to find, right? I mean, how many of them wear duffel coats these days? It's all crop tops and boob tubes and wee pelmet skirts wi' nae nickers. But she's no' like that. She's jist a wee lassie, a wee lost lassie. Say you'll do it. Joe says you're the best there is and I've kent Joe since we were mooching fags off the tally van thegither sixty years ago so I trust him. Say you'll do it."

Joe spoke before I could.

"I'll be covering the fee and your expenses," he said, immediately rendering me speechless for several minutes while the old lady continued.

"Jist fifteen, that's all she is. She shouldnae have been coming to the city on her ain; I've telt her and telt her that wolves eat cute wee rabbits here but will she listen? Will she hell. And noo look where it's got her. You'll dae it, won't you. You've got a kind face. Normally I don't go for that in a man, but I'll make an exception for you if you'll dae it."

I finally managed to get a word in edgeways, although I was still reeling from Joe's display of a previously deep hidden generosity.

"I only came in for a packet of fags, missus," I said. Joe slid two packs of Marlboro across the counter and waved away my twenty.

"On the house," he said.

That's when I knew it was serious.

I got the gen over a cup of strong sweet tea in Joe's wee room at the back of the shop—another indication that this was a day unlike any other. The green duffel coat belonged to the old lady's granddaughter, the girl was missing and I was being press-ganged into service, whether I liked it or not. But Joe was covering the fee, or rather, the fee was being covered by erasing my smokes tab in the shop and that was enough to make it worth my while for a couple of days.

When I told the old lady I'd help her out I got waterworks again so I left Joe to do the mopping up and took my new smokes out into the city to look for a duffel coated rabbit who had been lost among the wolves for nearly two days.

M y first port of call was in the city center and Queen's Street Station, the last known location of the girl. She'd come in by train from Stirling at five-fifteen, phoned her grannie on her mobile from the concourse to let her know they'd be together soon and then…nothing. Her phone wasn't answering, the police weren't interested and the grannie's tears were even now filling the teacups in Joe's back room.

I started by calling in a favor.

It's one of the perks of a long and slightly distasteful career as a P.I. in Glasgow; you end up knowing a lot of things that otherwise nice people would prefer kept quiet. Tommy McKinnely was a case in point. Five years ago he'd walked into a public lavatory in this very station and found a city councilor getting a handjob from a laddie too young to be out on his own. The councilor tried to get the polis to fit Tommy up. But before that could happen Tommy came to me, I found the young laddie and rather than Tommy getting shafted it was the councilor who ended up short in the wallet, to the laddie, to Tommy and inadvertently to me. Since then Tommy had stayed out of my way and our paths had no reason to cross; until now. As luck would have it, Tommy was on the security guard rota at Queen's Street station. If anyone could get me access to the CCTV footage it was Tommy. And as luck would again have it, he was on duty when I knocked on the office door.

H e refused to talk to me in the office but that was fine by me—it meant I could allow him to buy me a pint in the pub on the concourse. He had a tonic water, being on duty, but I made up for him by having a wee half of Bells to help the beer down; the first of the day and most welcome for it.

Tommy wasn't happy to be talking to me; I could see that just by counting his twitches. He was even less happy when I mentioned the lost lassie.

"I had that auld woman at me all day yesterday and all," he said, staring at his tonic water as if it was poisoned. "I'll tell you what I telt her. There's thousands of wee lassies pass through this place every day. We don't try to keep track of them."

"Aye, but the cameras do, don't they?"

He caught my gist; Tommy was smart, smart enough to have come to me after the thing in the lavvy. He wasn't quite smart enough to tell me to fuck off, which is what he should be doing at that point. Instead he gave me the spiel.

"It's more than my job's worth to let you see the footage, even if we kent where to look," he said.

"Oh, we ken where to look—she came off the quarter past five Stirling train, and she made a phone call on the concourse. We should be able to find her given that. And maybe we can see if anybody talked to her. That's all I need to know; I don't even need to see the footage. You can just tell me, describe anyone that she interacts with. I can take it from there and nobody needs to be any the wiser."

"I don't know, Derek, I…"

"You owe me, Tommy," I said, and let the thing lie there between us while I drank my whisky and he stared down his tonic water. Finally he went to get another round in and had a beer himself this time. That's when I knew I had him.

An hour later—an hour I spent in the bar getting another, slow, beer inside me—Tommy came up with the goods. He'd gone above and beyond—his words not mine—and produced a photie, sliding it face down across the table to me.

"It's a wee bit blurred. Our printer's fucked and the management's too bloody stingy to fix it but you can see clear enough. I found her right away, off the Stirling train as you said—and a mannie came up to her just after she got off the phone."

I turned the photo over to see a heavily built man, good suit, expensive overcoat, leading green duffel coat away with a protective arm around her shoulders.

"Then what?" I asked.

Tommy shrugged.

"Out the main exit past the ticket office and out of range. We used to have cameras on the taxi rank out there, but they're fucked too and naebody cares."

I tapped the photo.

"Any clues as to who this bugger is?"

Tommy shook his head.

"We've got plenty of resident pervs and letches but I ken

all of them. If he's a nonce, he's new around here."

My heart sank. Given the photie, chances were that green duffel coat was already spirited away to the evil dungeon of choice of the good suit and all I was likely to find was a body or at best a broken soul. Tommy surprised me by, at least partially, coming to my rescue.

"There's been rumors though," he said. "For the past few months. Lassies, all young, all off trains, all going missing and that. The polis ken about it, we were asked to keep an eye open and to report in."

"There's been nothing in the papers."

"No…keeping it quiet to avoid a scandal. It'll probably be councilors and the funny handshake brigade closing ranks again."

I tapped the photo.

"You'll have to tell them?"

"Aye. Now that I've found it, I'm not going to ignore it, not even for you, Derek. I need to be able to sleep at nights."

"I'm not asking you to ignore it. Could you give me a couple of hours of a head start though? That's all I'm asking. Leave it till five; give me a chance to get a lead on the wee lassie. If not for me, for the auld woman?"

I got my two hours and he got forty quid. Twenty quid an hour to keep your mouth shut isn't a bad way to come into money, especially when it was Old Joe that was paying, not me.

I finished my beer, hid the photo away in an inside pocket, and went for a walk to consider my next move.

G lasgow feels wrong to me in the heat, especially when the sun is beating down. The smell becomes more noticeable for one thing; old river, new shite, a toxic mix at the best of times. Then there's the fact that lads…and some lassies, roam the public areas 'taps aff', peely-wally flesh wobbling exposed where it would be better kept under a simmet. But mostly it's just me feeling my age, feeling cut off from the mob. It's a cliché, the man walking the dirty streets alone and tied for far too long to a job he neither likes nor understands, but it's one I've lived with for most of my adult life.

At least there's always beer and smokes. I had one of the latter on the suspension bridge while trying to decide to make a call that I knew would only cause trouble. Liz, Detective Sergeant out of Maryhill nick, and I have an on-off relationship, mostly off. And when we're on it's usually only when we're both drinking. Add in the fact that we both have a temper when the whisky hits the spot and you have a recipe for a hot mess. That's something I generally try to avoid when working. But I already knew the cops were ahead of me on at least some points of this case and Liz was the only cop I knew who would even talk to me.

I had another smoke before getting out the phone then took the plunge before I could talk myself out of it.

Her first words weren't encouraging.

"Fuck off, Derek. I don't have time for your shite."

"I bet you say that to all the boys."

"Only the ones that need to fuck off. Now are you going to take the hint or do I cut you off."

"Green duffel coat," I said, and heard the sigh at the other end of the line.

"The auld woman?"

"Aye, the auld woman. She's pally with old Joe."

"Probably after his Cornetto."

"Is that what we're calling it now?"

She sighed loudly again, just to make her point.

"We've been told to lay off," she said.

"Telt? By who?"

"It came from higher up than I'm allowed to think about," she replied. "So don't go stepping on any toes you shouldn't on this one. The shite will flow."

"And the wee lassie?"

There was only quiet for a time at the other end of the line before she spoke.

"If there was to be something through your letterbox that you might need to read, you might think it came from somebody with inside info, but you'd be wrong to think that. Capiche?"

I capiched. We talked for a bit more, nothing substantial but at least she didn't tell me to fuck off again so I was feeling in a better frame of mind when I headed home to check my mail.

T he package that definitely wasn't from somebody with inside info was lying just inside the main door. Whoever had left it had struggled to get it through the letterbox, the bundle of papers being thicker than the gap they needed to go through. Some of the outer pages were ripped and torn but at least I hadn't taken delivery of a fresh shite.

I made a pot of coffee, lit a smoke, and tried to peruse the papers quickly but I soon found that I'd been sent what, at first glance at least, were unrelated notes that had no apparent connection to a wee lassie from Stirling in a green duffel coat.

What there was proved to be a lot of stuff about the auction sale of an old mirror, alongside a potted biography of the mirror's original owner, an English toff in the early 18th

Century, Francis Dashwood, 11th Baron le Despencer. Along with that there was what looked to be a photocopy of the personal journal of a gentleman in the Edwardian era. The jackpot was at the back of the bundle, a series of photos of men in places around Glasgow, some with names written on the back in handwriting I wasn't supposed to recognize, others with questions written in the same hand.

One of the last ones I looked at seemed familiar and a closer inspection with a magnifying glass proved, to my own satisfaction at least, that the mannie in the photie was the same one who had escorted green duffel coat out of Queen's Street Station. In this one he was pictured going in to Glasgow City Halls in George Square. Unfortunately his was one of the unnamed pictures. The writing on the back just had a date and time, 4:30pm, 22nd March of this year. Others had dates stretching back to last year.

I couldn't make sense either of the texts or the photos, although I knew who some of the men—and they were all men—were in them. The connections between various city councilors, bookies, art dealers and football management eluded me for the moment. But I knew a man who knew a lot of men in the city.

And it was time for another pint anyway.

I stuffed my pockets with the paperwork where it would fit and headed where I'd meant to go hours ago.

T he Twa Dugs at the foot of Byres Road is more than a favorite watering hole. It also serves as the source of much of the information I get to help me on what's loosely classed as 'cases'.

Tonight was no exception. George, barman, owner and a man who kens where all the best bodies are buried, took one look at my pile of photographs and sucked at his teeth.

"You don't want to be messing with this lot, Derek. There's half the money in the city showing in these photies. Whatever you're after it's likely to be something they want to keep hidden."

"I suspect they're abducting wee lassies fresh off the trains at Queen's Street Station and having their evil ways with them," I said. "So I don't really gie a fuck how much money they've got. I've got one wee lass in particular to find for her grannie but it would be nice to send them all down at the same time."

"You don't just send lads like this down, Derek," George said, pouring me a pint of heavy. "You've been around the block often enough. You ken the score."

"Aye. Why is it I'm always two-nil down with a minute to go?"

"Money. Pure and simple. They've got it, we havenae. You ken that too."

"Aye. Same as it ever was. But I could use a wee bit of help if you can manage it? If you don't want to mess with them all, just give me one." I shuffled out the photo of the man I suspected of the abduction and tapped it. "If I can get at him I get a start and you can go back to forgetting about it. There's fifty quid for anybody who can lead me to him. Put the word out, see what the jungle drums say?"

He still wasn't too keen, and I could hardly blame him; quite a bit of the business George does under the counter probably passed through the hands of some of the men in the photos. I was asking him to take a chance with his livelihood. But I knew him well enough to know his views on predators of wee lassies and wasn't surprised when he made the photo disappear into a pocket.

"Have a pint. Have a few pints. I'll see what I can do."

I took up my usual seat in the corner away from the door. My auld pals, drinking partners and sources of gossip, Andy and Jock were over near the window playing draughts and slowly but surely taking all the money off a pair of fresh faced students slumming it for the night. Everybody else in the place was busy with the serious business of getting the drink inside them but I wasn't ready for that high-dive this early in the evening. Not when I was working.

By now Tommy would have passed the photo of the man at the station on to the Polis, maybe even to Liz herself, although given what she'd told me on the phone I wasn't holding out much hope of them doing anything with the information. My only chance was with George's network and whatever else I might find in the papers. I unearthed them from my jacket pockets, smoothed them out, and went over them more carefully than I had back in the flat.

The notice of the sale of an antique mirror, a sale that dated from here in Glasgow in the Nineteen-Twenties told me little more than it had come from somewhere called Medmenham Abbey and was thought to be over a hundred years old at the time of the sale. There was a post-it note stuck to the notice, and in that hand I still wasn't supposed to recognise a note read. *Mirror property of Dashwood?* At least somebody had been making connections. And Dashwood was a name I recognised from earlier. I shuffled through to the potted biography and read of a Lord of the manor, hellraiser, roisterer, seeker of sins, fornicator and rapist of the local peasantry, with a bunch of friends all into the same passions. There was also a name I finally recognised from some almost forgotten TV documentary--*The Hellfire Club.*

I was about to start in on the accompanying journal when a fresh pint of heavy arrived at my elbow and Andy and Jock sat down around the wee table.

"What are you working on, Derek?" Jock asked. Andy was busy counting fivers; he had quite a bundle of them and the two students were slipping sheepishly out the front door when I looked up.

"Nothing that makes as much as you pair of codgers. You should be ashamed of yourselves, taking money off babbies at your age."

"If they're daft enough to think we're daft enough to lose money to them, then we'd be daft not to take advantage of the fact." Jock replied, and while I was still trying to process the sentence he had leaned forward to pick up some of the papers in front of me. I just had enough time to get a wee bit of the good stuff—some of the photographs mainly—back into my pocket before their questions started. I yielded to the inevitable and went with the flow; once these two get started it's the only way to survive.

"The Hellfire Club, eh?" Jock said. "What are you doing reading up on that auld nonsense?"

"It might be relevant to a case," I said.

"And it might be bollocks," Andy replied. "There's a story that the Hellfire Club was a snow job; Dashwood was fitted up for it by political opponents. The man went on in later years to hold the post of Chancellor of the Exchequer and then other high offices in the colonies. That's hardly the life history of a debauched rake."

I laughed.

"Is there anything you two don't know something about?"

"It's the quiz nights," Jock laughed. "We've got a reputation to defend."

By now Andy had joined in on going through the papers. He latched on to the notice of sale of the mirror and the post-it note.

"Whoever wrote this might have been on to something. Medmenham Manor was where the Hellfire Club was supposed to have got started in the first place."

"I still don't see what it's got to do with the price of tatties, though," Jock added. "What's this in aid of, Derek? Anything we can be helping with?"

"Unless you ken anything about how the auction of a mirror a hunner years ago connects up with a gang of nonces here and now then…"

Andy interrupted.

"There was something about a mirror," he said to Jock, and suddenly I was ignored completely. "Back in the Sixties. You remember, when all that psychedelic shite was all the rage? "

George waved me over to the bar and saved me from falling down the rabbit hole of history with the two older men.

"I might have a man who can help you," he said.

A minute later I was out the door and headed for the town centre. As I paid for the cab at the other end I realised I'd left Jock and Andy with the rest of the paperwork.

19

2

G lasgow Central railway station is Queen's Street's older, more battered big brother. When I was a lad steam trains still ran under its high-vaulted, almost cathedral like roofs but it had long lost any of that vintage charm. There was only one ticketing booth open and the queue snaked across the whole width of the concourse. That, coupled with the fact that there'd been two big football matches in the city that afternoon and all four sets of fans were doing their ritual cock-strutting meant it wasn't exactly the best place for a quiet rendezvous. And the last man I expected to be there to meet me under the old clock was Tommy McKinnely.

He put up a hand to defend himself as I approached.

"I ken, I ken. Why didn't I mention it earlier, that's what you're thinking. But hear me out. I didnae recognize the fella in the CCTV footage. It was only when this got circulated that I kent him." He showed me a copy of the same photo I'd had George circulate, of the man on the City Hall steps. "As soon as I clocked this, I remembered him."

"And this isnae just a wee scheme to squeeze some more tenners out of me?"

"Honest to God, Derek. And to prove it, I'll tell you before you show me the money. He's Geordie Watkins, oot of Bellshill originally. Handy with his fists and works as muscle for Monaghan the bookie. I ken him because I saw him beat the shite out of Tommy Flanagan in the bogs of the Horseshoe for no' paying his debts a couple of years back."

"And where do I find him?"

"That's your job, isn't it? It's no' as if he asks me round for my tea. The word was that you jist wanted a name and that was worth fifty quid. So, are you a man of your word, Derek?"

Easy money comes and goes easy. Fifty quid went into Tommy's wallet to join the earlier forty and I left him heading for a bar to get rid of it as I went in search of a phone book.

I n these days of mobile phones it's less and less usual to find somebody the old fashioned way but my luck was in. There was only one George Watkins in the book, address listed in the West End in a flat in Oakfield Avenue. I took a number 59 bus back, sat up on top having a furtive smoke and considered my next move.

Obviously if he was the man I was after a direct approach wasn't likely to get me much more than a direct 'Fuck Off'. On the other hand there was the problem of time; the wee lassie had been missing too long already, too many hours among the wolves for her to be unscathed. I was still thinking about it when I got off the bus on Gibson Street and walked up the wee hill into Oakfield Avenue.

Once upon a time, when the world and I were both young, I too had lived in this street, a top floor flat with a handful of mates and one girlfriend, long deceased. I walked past what used to be our entranceway but didn't look up to see if a light was on; some memories stay buried for good reason. Instead I went along three more doors and up into the close and stairwell of number 119.

It was well kept in the old style, gleaming racing green

Victorian era tiles on the walls, clean stone stairs and firm black ironwork on the railing. The windows on each landing were still topped with their original stained glass semi-circles and high overhead the domed skylight still had its metal framework. It felt gentile, faintly expensive and much too cozy for the likes of a bookie's muscle.

He'd been listed in the book as Flat 6. That made it the top floor, on the left. I smelled it before I reached the last flight of stairs. My first thought was that there had been a chip pan fire; there was the same thick, oily residue hanging in the air. When I reached the door to number six it felt slightly warm to the touch but not overly so and there was no smoke when I lifted the letterbox and peered through into an empty hallway. I made a split second decision based on a hunch, the old Yale lock stood up for less than two seconds to my Jimmy, and I was inside with the door shut behind me another two seconds later.

The smell was far worse inside, thicker, meatier and enough to have me breathing shallowly through my mouth. I knew the layout immediately; bathroom and small bedroom to the left, main bedroom to the right, kitchen ahead to the left, living area to the right out the front of the building. I thought the smell must be from something burning on the stove but as I approached the far end of the hallway it was clear that the stench was emanating from the front room. And suddenly I wanted to be somewhere else entirely; even listening to old Jock and Andy ramble about the '60s would be preferable to taking another step.

It was the thought of the wee lassie in the green duffel coat that got me moving again. I stepped out of the hallway into the main living area.

Geordie Watkins, what was left of him, lay in the middle

of the floor in the room, lying on his back, fists raised in a pugilist's guard. But it wasn't his boxing skills that had brought him to that state, it had been the fire that had consumed him so utterly there was little left but a blackened shell. The stench was thick, almost chewable. I felt gorge threaten at the back of my throat and pushed it away while I quickly went around the room. I don't quite know what I was looking for.

All I knew was that I wasn't looking at the body.

There was nothing to be found in the living room nor in the rest of the flat to tell me where the wee lassie might be. If she'd been here she'd left no trace and Geordie Watkins wasn't going to be telling me.

It looked like a hit job to me; the only problem was I couldn't see how it had been done. The body was so badly gone that some kind of accelerant had to have been used but it lay on a carpet that showed no sign of even a singe and nothing else in the room was burned at all.

Still, that was a mystery for the cops to solve. All it was for me was a dead end.

As I turned to leave I thought I caught a movement in the mirror above the fireplace, red, like fire in a wind. When I turned to check the room there was still only the dead body on the floor and for a boxer he was being far too static.

I backed out of the flat making sure to run a handkerchief over everything I'd touched and was out on the street only ten minutes after going in. As far as I knew no one had paid any attention to me and I meant to keep it that way. I took a turn up the hill at the school and over Hillhead back down to Byres Road smoking a couple of cigarettes and not quite getting the acrid taste of the late Geordie Watkins out of my mouth.

23

I went into the underground station to a public phone, made an anonymous call in an atrocious accent to the cops, then headed south for The Twa Dugs and a much needed drink.

S o there I was, fifty quid lighter and nowt to show for it but a dead man and a dead end. Back in the Dugs Andy and Jock tried to catch my eye as soon as I got in but I went straight to the bar for a quiet word with George. Over a pint I brought him up to speed on my meeting at Central Station and the finding of the dead thing on the floor in Oakfield Avenue. He sucked his teeth.

"Monaghan's muscle? And you're sure he's the one that took the wee lassie?"

"Tommy was sure. And the fact that it looks like Watkins got taken out just after I put the word out that I was looking for him tells me that somebody is covering their tracks."

"So what's your next move?"

"Monaghan?" I said, and George sucked his teeth again. Three times in a day; I must have him worried.

"Yon's a slippery bag of shite," he advised me. "Make sure you don't put both feet in it."

"Is he still in the big hoose in Kelvinside?"

"Last I heard, aye. There's a new blonde in tow wi' even fewer brain cells than the last one and the ex-wife is shacked up wi' a lawyer from down in one of the posh flats in the Merchant City. Monaghan's a man of habit. Saturday night he'll be in his conservatory, making sure the day's money was counted properly. Later he'll have a wee whisky or two, then he'll be way to bed wi' the new blonde."

"How do you ken so much about him?"

"I keep an eye on the competition," George said deadpan.

"If it helps, I don't have a scooby what they get up to in the bedroom; my curiosity only extends so far."

"And if I wanted a quiet word with him, with no chance of interruption?"

"He'll be covered. Two men at least. And if it wasn't him that wasted Watkins, he'll have heard about it by now and will be spooked, so you can expect him to have called in the heavy mob for protection."

"So my best chance is to keep an eye on him, see which way he jumps?"

"That's the safe choice."

"Aye, well, you ken me."

"Take care, Derek. These are not nice men."

"If I need somebody to hold my jacket, I'll shout."

I took three beers over to the table where Andy and Jock were sitting to see why they were so keen to catch my attention.

Andy waved a sheaf of my paperwork in my face.

"I don't suppose you want to tell us where you got this, Derek?"

"I don't even know what it is, never mind where it came from," I replied, handing out the beers and sitting down.

"It's pure fiction," Jock said disdainfully as he took a long sip of beer that left a mustache of foam on his upper lip. "A pile of shite, that's what it is."

"But it backs up the story from the Sixties," Andy replied. "You can see that."

"I can see fuck all," Jock replied. "This is your theory, not mine. You tell him."

"Aye, Andy. Go on, tell me, put me out of my suspenders."

"Jock and I have been talking," he began, and I laughed.

"Tell me something I don't know."

"Do you want this story or not? I could always be over at the window seat taking money off smooth-faced weans rather than taking to a cranky big bastard like you."

"Naw, goan yoursel' auld man. I'm listening."

He poked at the auction sale notice for the mirror. "It all comes down to this," he said. "But first, some history. I've done some digging on that there internet in your absence and I think I've got the facts in the right order."

"Facts? Is that what we're calling pish now?" Jock said, but Andy ignored him.

"There's a story of the Hellfire Club, of a cursed mirror and a ritual that called up Auld Nick himself to give 'advice' to the club members at their command."

"See," Jock said with a snort that finally dislodged the foam from his lip. "Pish."

"Whether it's pish or not bears no nevermind to the story," Andy replied. His finger moved to poke at the pages of the journal.

"A hunner years later, the mirror turns up in London, in the hands of a dabbler in occult studies, the writer of this journal if it is to be believed."

"Charlatan," Jock said.

"Investigator," Andy countered, and Jock decided it wasn't worth the argument as Andy picked up one of the pages and read aloud.

"The effort involved in moving the heavy mirror into the parlour and the lack of sleep the night before, finally caught up with me. I slumped into my chair, exhausted, barely having the strength to get a pipe lit and going. From the chair, and given the angle at which I had leaned the mirror against the wall, I only saw my

slippered feet reflected in the glass, and the patterned rug beneath stretching away from me into the distance.

"In my tiredness I was lost in a reverie, just sucking smoke and letting my mind drift, so if was some time before I realised that there was something happening in the reflection, and, by Jove, it gave me such a fright. As I looked in the mirror I saw a red fire creep towards my feet, tendrils of flame like a nest of snakes crawling forward to grip around my ankles.

"I was up and out of the chair so fast that I dropped my pipe at my feet. To my astonishment it did not show in the reflection, where the forest of flame continued to grow. Even now it crept up my shins, reaching for my knees. And as if in response I began to feel a great burning sear my limbs.

"I left at a run for the dining room, returning with a tablecloth which I threw over the glass. Immediately the heat dissipated, melting away as quickly as it had come. I smelled burning, but it was only my dropped pipe, which had spilled ash on the rug, ash which continued to smoulder."

"Burning," Andy said. "Just like in the '60s. You see?"

"Clear as mud, auld yin," I replied. "You havnae telt me about the '60s yet."

"I'm getting to it. But there's more of this guy yet, just a wee bit…" He read again.

"I set my electric pentacle to overlay the drawn pentagram upon the floor, seven glass vacuum circles -- the red on the outside of the pentacle, and the remainder lying inside it, in the order of orange, yellow, green, blue, indigo and violet. This particular order of colours had proved most efficacious during my adventure in the Larkhill Barrow, and I felt sure that it would once again serve me well with this particular problem. When I connected up the battery, a rainbow glare shone from the intertwining vacuum tubes. Content that my protections were in place I detached the pentacle from the battery and made for the scullery, for I knew that if I were to face any denizens from the Outer Regions, it would be best to be fully fortified in advance.

"I made a hearty meal of potatoes and cold meats that I found in the larder, and washed it all down with a bottle of Fuller's London Porter, which in itself was enough to fortify me for the day. I washed up the plates and was about to brew a pot of tea when I heard the first voices waft in from the library. As I headed in that direction I noticed that night was falling outside. I only just remembered in time to snatch my pipe and tobacco pouch from the parlour. Once back in the library I pulled the cloth away from the mirror, reattached the battery and entered the pentacle.

"As I sat cross legged inside the safe zone I could make out voices raised around me, but as yet it was little more than a loud whisper and I could discern no detail. At first all I saw in the mirror was my own reflection but shortly other images formed, as if painted in to the scene, strangely clothed men and women laughing and joking. My own image sat among them, but they walked through me as if it was I who was the phantasm. I sat there, astonished, as a whole night's festivities of the Hellfire Club replayed itself before me, as if I were watching a recording not just of sound, but also of vision.

"I will not bore you with the vile debauchery or the lewd and libidinous conduct on show. Suffice it to say that my theories as to the amateur nature of the hellish Club were more than confirmed. It did however raise a question in my mind as to how such a band of mindless seekers after carnal pleasures managed to get recorded in such a manner.

"I was on my third pipe by the time my question was answered.

"It began almost imperceptibly. A voice, far way in the background, started to intone a chant. I could scarcely make it out amid the sound of frenzied coupling that seemed to be all around *me. However the azure crystal on my pentacle flared and pulsed in time with the new voice, also showing me that there might be some external manifestation of the mirror's power.*

"A tall, well built man strode forward, wandering amid the frolics, reading from a large book he held in front of him. It was obvious from his expression that he felt he was having a bit of fun but I was starting to recognise pieces of what he said, and a deep fear crawled within me.

"The words being spoken formed a ritual that is mentioned in the Sigsand MS alongside dire warnings against its use, for it summons entities from the Outer Planes to come to the bidding of the speaker. And, of course, such a thing is not to be done lightly... and certainly not by dabblers like those in the Hellfire Club. I sat, pipe cooling and forgotten, as the gathered revellers inside the mirror came to realise the extent of their predicament. Flickering flames gathered, in the distance at first, then with great speed coming into the foreground, slithering, snake-like among the now fearful revellers. Screams broke the sudden silence as the red tendrils surged. Soon the whole view was engulfed in squirming fire, and the screams died away, first to pleading whimpers, then to a dead silence that was perhaps more frightening still."

"You see?" Andy said, pleading with both Jock and me. "Fire again. Fire then, fire in the '60s too."

"And fire now," I added. That got both their attentions as I went on. "I think I'd better hear about the thing in the '60s. You can let me decide whether it's shite, pish or neither."

A ndy was looking at some scribbled notes in the wee book he kept in his pocket for charting horses' form at the bookies.

"There's just a wee bit more background info first, just to keep things on the timeline straight."

He found what he was looking for and continued.

"The writer of the journal did some hocus-pocus with what he called his electric pentacle, and he seemed to think he'd, in his words, *cleansed the residue of the Outer Darkness.* The mirror turns up again here in Glasgow in Nineteen Twenty, so it looks like they lost interest in it down south. There was plenty of interest at the auction though."

He checked his notes again.

"That was where yon internet came in handy. It went for nearly three hunner pound, which in the Twenties was a shitload of cash. Or should I say a shipload, for it went to one of the Lords of the Clyde, Sir Peter Feltingham, big in shipping, timber and steel and, if rumour is to believed, serial fornicator of wee, and by wee I mean young, lassies. Any of this making sense to you yet, Derek?"

"I'm getting there. Go on."

"Well, there the trail goes cold for forty-odd years. I presume the mirror sat on a wall gathering dust in his Lordship's big hoose in Perthshire. But something of its connection with the Hellfire Club survived, if the thing in the '60s is to be believed."

"For God's sake," Jock said, waving an almost empty glass in the air. "Get the fuck on with it. I'm gasping here."

"I'll make it short and sweet then," Andy said. "In the late '60s, when all that LSD, tuning in dropping out shite was rife and Mick Jagger was droning on about sympathy for the devil, a group of lads, nearly in their twenties but no more than wee boys really, took it into their heads to call up the devil. They found four of them dead by burning the next morning and the other two never left the psychiatric wards after that.

"Here's where you come in, Derek. The focus of their wee

ceremony was said to be an old mirror famous in family stories and the instigator of the whole fiasco was young Anthony Feltingham, grandson of the mannie who bought the Hellfire mirror at auction. Join the dots, hey presto, and Robert's your maw's brother."

"Aye. All well and good," I replied. "But I don't see how it helps now."

Andy tapped at the paperwork.

"Somebody's been putting the clues thegither. It's time you helped out, don't you think?"

"So this mirror, where is it now?"

Andy shrugged.

"Unheard of since the affair in the '60s."

"Then Jock was right. Your story's pish," I said, smiling to show I didn't really mean it. "The only common factor is the burning."

I told them about Geordie Watkins.

"This just confirms it. I'm betting somebody's found the mirror and has worked out how to use it," Andy said.

"Use it? You use it to have a shave in the morning and check your teeth for spinach," Jock said. "How else do you use a bloody mirror."

I went to the bar to get a round in for them, both to avoid what looked like an incoming argument and to make a start at processing the information that was coming at me faster than my brain could handle. I had no idea what I meant to do next but George's words to me as he handed over the beers gave me a push in a direction I thought I might be able to follow.

"I had somebody check Monaghan out for you, Derek," he said. "He's home, with four tooled up goons on the doors, so he's scared of something. You get a grand view of his conservatory from the big chestnut tree on the other side of his back garden wall. There's a pair of binoculars and a flask of coffee up in the crook of the branches if you want to use them. Your choice."

It was indeed and I made it. Jock and Andy got a beer each and a spare to wash them down and I caught a taxi to Kelvinside.

Monaghan's house was one of those big blousy Victorian things that the gentry built back then to prove that they were better than rank and file Glasgow folk. Monaghan was using it today for much the same purpose, adding his own particular garish touches such as a glasshouse swimming pool, a putting green and more pampas grass than can be found in South America.

The place was lit up as if for Christmas and there was an armed man in the garden outside the conservatory less then twenty yards from me. I felt for sure that my position ten feet up in the chestnut tree just over the garden wall must be clear for all but a blind man to see. But nobody took any note of me and I was able with the use of the wee pair of binoculars to get a close up view of a very worried man.

He was at a desk facing out towards the garden, working at a laptop, writing furiously, and punctuating each full stop with a vicious swig at a whisky bottle. I hoped he didn't have too many sentences to go, for at the rate he was getting through the Scotch it wasn't going to be long before he couldn't see never mind type.

After a while he hit a button hard, almost punching the keyboard, and turned around. I followed his gaze to see to pieces of paper come out of a printer in the corner. I had leaned forward for a closer look, forgot about the thermos flask that was between my knees, and lost it. It fell clattering down through the branches and a flashlight beam picked me out as if I was transfixed by a spotlight on stage.

"Don't mind me," I said as the guard came towards me. "I'm just up here looking for my cat."

Then I was clambering, almost dropping, heading for the ground and a run for safety.

It wasn't to be. The heavy in the garden had pals, several of them, and they caught me before I'd got twenty yards. I didn't throw any punches, put my hands up and offered to come quietly. They knocked me about a bit anyway but I was able to walk, albeit with a bit of a limp, when they herded me towards the conservatory.

M onaghan was still working hard on the whisky and it took him a few seconds to focus on me.

"You're no polis," he said. "I ken you. You're that big saft shite, the wee pretendy detective fae Byres Road. That's you, isn't it?"

"You got me fair and square," I said. "That's me. I only came around to see if you've seen a green duffel coat."

"Oh, I ken why you're here," Monaghan said and took another deathly swig of Scotch. "You put the word out about Geordie Watkins, Geordie got malkied, and it's my turn next. And it's your fault. I've got four men down in Partick looking to break your legs right now, and here you are, pretending to be a big man and sweating on ma carpet."

"I'm just looking for a wee lassie."

"That's the problem, isn't it? That's what this is all aboot, some wanker looking for a wee lassie. I should never have got involved in the first place, never got Geordie to do their dirty work for them. Worse than the fucking masons this lot."

I thought about my answer to that one. I was playing for

time. The big lad on my left side looked to be itching to hit me again and I didn't intend to let him. That suggested that a lot of violence would be visited on me from his pals and I wanted to avoid that for as long as possible. So I hit Monaghan with a hunch to see how he'd react.

"Well, that's what you get for fucking with the owner of a cursed mirror, isn't it? What did you think you'd get out of it, tea and scones at the vicarage?"

Monaghan suddenly looked sober, his gaze fixed on me without the out-of-focus look it had seconds earlier.

"Who said anything about a fucking mirror? I never said anything about a fucking mirror, did I?" He looked to his henchmen for confirmation that they were only too happy to provide, given that a small handgun had appeared in his right hand and he was waving it around alarmingly. "What do you know about the fucking mirror? That's a secret."

"A funny handshake, trousers rolled up in one leg kind of secret, or the kind of secret that gets wee lassies wearing green duffel coats fed to the wolves kind of secret?" I asked.

He went quiet at that.

"Who kens you're here?" he said softly.

"Everybody I spoke to in the pub before coming here, the taxi driver that brought me here, the polis, the wifie in the shop where I bought my fags, your big pals here, you and me. And anybody else that's watching you."

I don't know what I said that last bit; I wondered what might happen if I fuelled his obvious worry rather than try to defuse it, add some chaos into the mix. I didn't expect it to be quite so explosive as it turned out though.

He got in my face with the gun.

"What do you mean by that? Who else is watching me?"

"How the fuck would I know? It's your hoose."

He smacked me, hard, on the jaw with the butt of the gun. I staggered but didn't go down; he wasn't that big a man and the whisky had softened his edge. It would still hurt to speak after it though and the pain ran from chin to the crown of my skull, setting my head ringing like a struck bell.

He turned to the heavy on my right, the one who'd been out in the garden earlier.

"You, you should be ootside, no' fucking about like a wet fart in here. Get oot there and do your fucking job."

It was when the big man turned to go that it happened. I saw it first because I was looking over Monaghan's shoulder, directly at a large mirror on the far wall beside the door to the main house. It was only a flicker but I'd seen its like before, in Watkins flat and I remembered the words that Andy had read from the old journal.

Flickering flames gathered, in the distance at first, then with great speed coming into the foreground.

It was just like that, a fire spreading fast but only inside the mirror, the reflection of the conservatory being consumed in flame while we in the actual conservatory were untouched. Monaghan hadn't noticed. He looked like he was winding up to hit me again so I nodded toward the mirror.

"Looks like somebody was watching you after all."

He turned, let out a wail of terror and raised the pistol. I think he was intending to shoot the mirror, to break it before the flames escaped. But it was already too late. A thin line of fire no wider than a finger leapt out from the mirror's surface and not burning the carpet across which it flashed reached Monaghan's toes. It immediately started to consume him, flowing up him in a whole body caress that set his clothes bursting aflame. He tried to scream. It burned his tongue, washed down his throat, and he was dead before he fell, flames in his eye sockets, flames in his mouth, flames at his ears.

He hit the carpet hard and lay still.

The heavies decided they were having no more part of it and took to their heels. I joined them, but made a detour via the printer first. I was worried that a delay might mean the fire got to me but it wasn't paying me any interest. The line of flame retreated the way it had come, still not burning the carpet, was sucked back into the mirror and everything went in reverse, the flames dying away as quickly as they had come. The only thing I saw now in the reflection was my already bruising face and the dead body at my feet.

I pocketed the two sheets of paper and left the way I'd come in.

The heavies were nowhere to be seen.

3

T here's never a taxi around when you need one. I started
walking, and was almost at the top end of Byres Road
before the first cab passed me, going the wrong way and
with its meter down.

I'd stopped looking for a ride by then in any case, chain
smoking and trying to process what I'd just seen. It looked
like Andy's theory of the mirror being involved might be the
right one after all. The idea that it might be possible wasn't
giving me all that much pause for thought; it wasn't as if I
didn't have previous when it came to fucking about with
dodgy mirrors.

And as soon as that thought came I knew where I had to
go next; a return to a crime scene, but not one related to
tonight. Ten minutes later I was walking up Hyndland Road,
heading for the sigil house.

It was getting late by then but I wasn't worried; the
concierge kept similar hours to me, and I'd never yet been
denied entry. Tonight was no exception. She showed me into
her wee room and gave me a glass of some very expensive
Scotch, a wee ritual we'd fallen into, a chat before I went up to
the room.

"This isn't a routine visit," I said as I lit up one of her
Gauloise to change the taste in my mouth. "I'm here because

of a mirror."

I told her the story, she took it all in, then shook her head slowly.

"I cannot help you with this, Derek, you know that. I only know this house, its secrets."

"I guessed as much. But it helped to talk to you about it anyway. Now I know what I'm going to say when I get upstairs."

I headed up. The door opened by itself to let me in.

I wasn't surprised.

A sofa and a mirror, those were the room's only contents. I sat on one and looked into the other. Once upon a time, in this very room, I'd helped a woman I might have loved kill a bad man. We'd both taken a trip to the other side of the big mirror that stood in the middle of the floor. I'd come back. She hadn't and as far as I knew she was still in there somewhere. Every so often I come here and talk to her. She'd never yet replied, but I always have hope, more so after tonight, for if mirror magic was working in one place, it might well work in another.

I sat and smoked and I talked, not about the case at first, private stuff, between the two of us. After a while the room grew colder but it was just the night air and the mirror showed only my own face. The bruise on my chin was going to be a brammer in the morning and the pain was already reminding me that I needed more booze but I sat for a bit longer.

After a time I remembered the two sheets of paper. I got them out of my pocket where they'd got rumpled. I flattened them with my hand and read.

Monaghan had written it as an anonymous note, intended

for the polis. It had that overblown, slightly formal, tone of someone not used to writing, trying to sound intelligent and serious.

To whom it may concern

Some information has come into my possession regarding the recent abductions of young girls from the city's railway terminals, and it is my duty as a concerned citizen to make this information available to the constabulary.

I must point out that I am an innocent in this matter, having had the information passed on to me in the course of a business meeting by someone with inside information, someone who knew the details of the operation and has now paid the ultimate price for it.

That man's name was George Watkins and it is the news of his demise today that has led me to pen this note.

I spoke to George two days ago and he told me his concerns of a job he was doing for a prominent Glasgow businessman. This job involved George in procuring women for parties that this man hosts in a manor house in Perthshire whose name George was not ready to reveal to me.

George, by his own admission, freely procured prostitutes for the man for a period of some months. But of recent weeks the man's requests became more urgent, and more urgently for ever younger – fresher was the word George used – girls. George was offered money, a very large amount of money, and it went to his head.

And it was George who was responsible for the disappearance of the girls, always taken from railway stations, never to be seen again.

George would not reveal to me the name of the businessman but I understand, from injudicious hints George has dropped while in his cups, that the Perthshire house is just to the north of Pitlochry.

The responsible man should not be hard to find and I urge you to track him down, for although George is dead, the parties are still ongoing.

More girls will disappear if you ignore this note and their blood will be on your hands,

A concerned citizen.

He'd given them just enough info to give the polis something to go on and not enough to give himself away. Not a bad job by a man with so much whisky in him.

There was a P.S. I almost didn't notice it at first because he'd put in a dozen or so line feeds before adding it at the bottom of the second page.

P.S. They dump these wee lassies in a crypt in the Necropolis. Fourth row out from the Cathedral, north end. Their mothers and faithers deserve to ken.

I was up and out of the sofa heading for the door two seconds later. As I reached the door I heard a soft voice speak to me. When I looked back the mirror was showing only the room.

I know what she said though, I know she was there. That gives me hope for the next time.

"Good luck, Derek."

By rights I should have gone directly to Liz with the letter and the bombshell P.S., but I had the bit between my teeth and I had a lassie's grannie to think about. If green duffel coat was lying dead in an open grave, I wanted to be the one to find her. Well, I didn't really, but you know what I mean. It's one of those things a man who's gotta do things has gotta do. Or something like that.

I was fed up with running about town and getting socked in the jaw though. I got a taxi outside Tennent's Bar in Byres Road and let the driver talk at me about immigrants for twenty minutes till we got to the city centre. I got my own back by paying him and not giving him a tip. I listened to him curse me out long and loudly as I walked away, heading for the Cathedral.

It was late by then, around midnight, and I was aware I hadn't brought a torch. I was heading into a graveyard used by people who dump dead bodies with impunity and I was armed only with my wits and harsh language. I resolved to use as much of both as I could muster and headed up the hill.

The Necropolis is one of these places with a reputation about having a reputation; around here they really know where the bodies are buried, and have been buried for hundreds of years. Generations of lads have brought lassies up here in the hope of scaring their hands up skirts, or brought pals up here with fags and lager or, increasingly these days, glue of something stronger in the hope of chasing oblivion. But tonight my luck was in, I had the place to myself, although that didn't make me feel any better as I made for the fourth row out.

As I got farther from the lit-up cathedral itself the shadows crept closer and darker around me and I travelled back a few of those hundred years back to a more superstitious hindbrain that knew better than to fuck about in a graveyard after midnight. On another night I would have turned on my heels and headed for a bottle but I had the wee lassie big in my mind, and keeping her to the forefront kept me moving forward.

I found the crypt I was looking for easily enough once I reached the north end; all I had to do was follow my nose.

I t had been a warm day, hot sun beating down on an enclosed crypt and the pale things that had been dumped in there had taken the heat into them and turned it rapidly into corruption. By the time I reached the iron grille door of the crypt the smell was overpowering. I had no intention of fucking about with the old heavy lock. I took out a handkerchief, covered my mouth and putting my back into it tore the grille out of the old stone in which it was fixed.

I won't dwell on what I found inside, I'll leave it to your imagination, just as it will give my own imagination a workout several nights a month in my dreams until only the whisky will help.

There were six of them, six young naked lassies in various stages of long gone and when I stumbled back out into the night gasping for air I was holding a green duffel coat in my left hand.

It was now most definitely time for the polis. I put a call in to Liz and sat a hundred yards upwind of the crypt smoking while waiting for the flashing lights and heavy boots to turn up.

O f course they were intent on fingering me as the bad guy in the situation; it's a lot easier to fit up somebody found in the vicinity of six dead bodies that it is to do the leg work to find the actual killers. They got even more exited when I told them where to find Monaghan, given that I was already confessing to being there when he died.

But that was as far as they got; I didn't tell them I'd been in Geordie Watkins' flat, Liz vouched for my credentials and try as they might over several hours in Maryhill nick they couldn't get me to change my story. There was plenty I didn't tell them of course; how do you tell cops about fire pouring out of mirrors and two hundred-year old satanic cults emergent in the city? I kept it simple; cops like simple because it matches their brains.

I knew the tech bods would be able to match the two

pages and the printing on them with Monaghan's printer and that they'd find more evidence on the bookie's laptop. I knew that they knew about Monaghan's connection with Watkins and even they could add two and two. I also knew they'd likely try to fit Monaghan and Watkins up together for the wee lassies and never mind that didn't explain how they both ended up burned to death. I could imagine the Chief Constable up on telly talking about a job well done and the double suicide of the suspects as the cordon was closing in. That's the way it's done, the way it's always been done, and it's the reason I'm a P.I. not a cop, for I can only take so much of being sick to my stomach and I'd rather the cause be whisky than my conscience.

By the time they were done with me it was after three in the morning and they let me out with the 'don't leave town' spiel that every cop's been using since Wyatt Earp.

Liz saw me to the door.

"We've got preliminary forensics," she said on the steps as I lit up my first smoke in hours. "She's not there."

"What do you mean she's not there. I found her coat didn't I?"

"Aye, you did. But it was another lassie that was wearing it. Your girl's a brunette. All six in that charnel pit tonight were blondes."

"So she might still be alive?"

"Your guess is as good as mine. But leave it, Derek. The cover up is already well on its way; investigation complete, shut the file, mark it up as a job well done and move on. You ken the drill."

"Aye, I ken the drill. But the fucker that actually did the lassies in is still out there, still up to fuckery, and I'll get him. I can go places you lot can't—you ken that too, that's why you sent me the paperwork."

"What paperwork?" she said, not for the first time reminding me never to play her at poker, for she looked like she meant it.

I got home at sometime around four, poured a large whisky, knocked it back and was asleep in the chair two minutes later.

I woke to Sunday morning sunshine. The fact that it wasn't accompanied by a hangover was something new but the aches and pains in my back made up for that. I had a token wash and change, decided not to bother shaving and went back out to meet the world.

Only, instead of the world, there was the old lady. She was in Joe's shop when I went in to replenish my fag supply and the waterworks were in full flow again.

"The polis say they've found bodies. Bodies they say. And you were supposed to find her and bring her back to me. Bodies."

It took me several minutes to convince her about the blonde/brunette thing. I didn't mention that I'd been the one who found the bodies and I definitely didn't mention the green duffel coat for that would surely have put her over an edge from which there would be no recovery. I had her in my arms by this time, and Joe only laughed when I looked pleadingly over her head for help.

She finally let go some minutes later; I was sure she'd added some new bruises to the ones the chair had inflicted.

"So she's still alive?"

I could have told her the truth, that I had no idea, that chances were that there were more of those bodies yet to be found and that the odds were stacked against her granddaughter. But she was a little old lady in distress and as I've already said, I'm putty in their hands.

"She's still alive. And I'll find her," I said, trying to copy Liz's way with a poker face from the night before. I saw that I hadn't convinced Joe but the old lady only needed somebody to confirm her hopes and I'd managed that well enough.

I got two more packs of fags without having to pass any money over the counter, left the old lady with another promise that she'd see her girl again, and went in search of the info that might help me manage to keep that promise.

T he Twa Dugs on a Sunday morning is much like The Twa Dugs at any other time apart from the fact that George gets some free crisps and peanuts put on the bar and lets one of his barmen run the session while he has a lie in. Some of the usual clientele don't turn up, being still in recovery from the night before. Jock and Andy, however, were in their drinking seat; they had Sundays off from rooking students and spent it on the serious business of getting beer inside them.

I got a round in, bowed to the inevitable again, and brought them up to date with all that had happened since I'd left the evening before. As was the way of things, Jock was incredulous while Andy soaked it all in.

"You actually saw the bad fire?" Andy said and the way he said it brought the memory back; my mother beating ten bells out of me after catching me smoking at age twelve and telling me that I'd 'go to the bad fire'. From Andy's tone I'm guessing his own mother had told him much the same thing.

"Aye," I replied. "And I saw it take the bad man. It's no' something I'm looking to repeat. But I've telt you my story. There's something I need from you…"

Andy interrupted me.

"Joseph, Joe, Sullivan, lawyer."

"What?" I said, and closed my mouth from where it had dropped open.

"Monaghan's wife's new fancy man down in the Merchant City and I'm guessing Monaghan's way up the social ladder."

"And what's he got to do with it?" I asked, but I already knew he was going to have everything to do with it.

"Only that he bought Hellvellen House in Perthshire, just north of Pitlochry a couple of years back. Bought it off the skint and on their uppers Feltingham family for a small fortune, with all contents included—I'm guessing that included all the auld mirrors. Rumour has it that he holds some pretty wild parties out there in the sticks where nobody will pay much attention. The internet is a truly wonderful thing for an auld man like me. It gets me free beer…or is that not worth a pint?"

It certainly was. I went to the bar again and got another round in; no worries, Old Joe was still paying after all.

Over the beer I didn't get much more info than they had given me already. There was more stuff on Sullivan, including the fact that he was one of the photos that I'd now made into a pile on the table and that most of the other photos were of people in his social circle or on the fringes of it.

"Connections," Andy said. "The world's full of them if you ken where to look."

"I'll connect my haun wi' the back of your heid if you don't get your round in," Jock replied.

I turned down the offer of another beer when Andy made it. It was time to be going.

I'd have liked to have had a wee word with George before

leaving, maybe arranging some backup muscle in case things got ugly, but George's Sunday's off were considered sacrosanct. No business was to be done until after five in the afternoon and I intended to be at the Perthshire house well before then.

I had a train to catch.

G oing to Pitlochry from Glasgow on a summer Sunday isn't as much fun as it might sound. It's easily enough done but it's not cheap and it takes a fuck of a long time. The Glasgow to Perth leg started slowing at Dunblane and I'd lost the will to live by the time we crawled though Gleneagles then flopped, hot and exhausted, into Perth Station. That's when I found that the connecting service had fucked off without me and there was a three hour long wait for the next one. There's not a lot for a grown man like me to do on a hot Sunday afternoon going on early evening in Perth besides drink so I went and did that.

I was hoping to make it slightly more palatable by giving the station bar a swerve and heading up the road for a more salubrious establishment. But all the local bars had a football match on; same match, different bars for the sets of opposing supporters to keep the later fights out of the hotels and on the streets. I had three noisy pints in one and two even noisier pints in another and by the time I got back to the railway station my head was ringing with tribal chants and my belly was swimming in sour beer.

Then the next Pitlochry train was late.

It was half past eight, eight hours after leaving Glasgow, before we crawled into Pitlochry. A sensible man would have got a room in a B&B for the night, got himself fortified with a meal and made a start on investigations in the morning.

Luckily, I am not a sensible man. I found an open off-license and got directions to Hellvellen House, two packs of fags, three bars of chocolate and a half bottle of whisky.

I was prepared for a stake out.

4

This wasn't my first rodeo, not even my first big country house stakeout. I've had a few of those over the years, the first of which was on the case that gave me my first brush with weird shit; that bloody Johnson amulet. As I walked the dark, overhung avenue towards Hellvellen house I was hoping I could at least get out of this particular case without everyone else involved either dying, going insane or being dragged headlong into another dimension. Good times.

I found Hellvellen House easily enough; it had its name on the gate, although the gate itself was shut, well lit up, of new thick iron and had some nasty looking spikes along the top that I wasn't willing to risk. I saw that there were lights on somewhere up the head of a long tree lined drive—it looked like somebody was home.

I walked the perimeter, looking for a safe place to clamber over. Some of these big houses utilise all the latest security mod cons from cameras to motion sensors. Others have a pack of Dobermann Pinchers trained to go for the goolies, while yet others employ ex-cops to spend five minutes every two hours walking the grounds. Hellvellen House had none of those, and that made me very twitchy.

I found a quiet spot and scrambled up on top, sitting there for a minute with my feet dangling on the outside of the wall so that I could drop down and get off and away at any sign of an alarm being raised. No bells rang, no dogs came looking for a tasty morsel, no ex-cops arrived looking to work off their bacon roll habit by beating me to a pulp. Twinkling lights from the house showed through the trees and I heard a distant hint of music in the air.

I dropped down off the wall and started a slow creep toward the house through the rampant rhododendron bushes. It still wasn't full dark yet although it was getting there quickly and I was able to keep to deep shadows and move slowly and as quietly as this disorganised body of mine would allow.

By the time I reached the edge of the shrubbery stars were showing in the sky although it would take a while yet for the heat of the day to dissipate. I chose a spot where I had a view of the front of the house, sidled up close to a welcoming tree and settled myself for the duration.

The house itself was bigger even than I'd expected, one of those huge rambling piles that would give Gormenghast a run for its money, all Victorian baronial style turrets, bay windows, cascading balconies and even a couple of gurning gargoyles that peered balefully across an expanse of lawn at me.

The twinkling lights I'd seen earlier were mostly coming from the largest window, tall French doors open to the night onto a granite patio and sweeping steps down to an overly lit fountain that sent soft hissing spray into the night air.

The sound of music was louder here too, an old jazz thing from the fifties that I should have recognised but wouldn't come to me. I felt my excitement grow, wondering if I'd coincidentally come along just as one of the parties was getting going. But there didn't seem to be much movement in the large room, certainly no indication that there was a crowd in there. Every so often a figure, a heavy built man, would get up, walk in front of the light, then back again a minute later; a drinker filling his glass was my guess. There was no sign of anyone else in the house.

I gave it twenty minutes then started to make my way round the back, looking for a way in. I'm not totally daft though; before I left my hiding place I made a quiet call to George's voice mail, telling him where I was and what I was up to, just in case I made it inside but not back out again.

I hadn't come with burglary in mind; I didn't even have my wee wallet of tools to hand and I wasn't dressed for creeping about quietly inside a rich man's house. But it looked so quiet in there and the thought of the young lassie was so big in my mind that I acted on instinct without trying to overly think matters. It was a chance I had to take, for it might never be so easy again.

I stayed in the shadows of the trees, gave the fountain a wide berth on the opposite side of it from the house and made my way round the right hand side of the property. Once there I had to skirt a large walled garden and an even larger greenhouse that contained an ostentatious swimming pool that would have had the bookie Monaghan green with envy.

The back of the house was like the back of most houses— less salubrious than the front, mostly business, with rubbish bins and staff car parking. The grassy areas here had an unkempt feel that told me the groundskeeper was more interested in keeping the boss happy than in doing a good job. There was only one car in the parking area, a battered old Land Rover. I hoped that meant they were running on minimal workforce; that would make my illicit creeping about all the easier.

There was a light on in what I took to be the kitchen, so there was no entry for me through the main back door. But my luck was in a few minutes later as I turned to the left side of the house and found an old coal cellar, unlocked and with steps leading down into a dark basement.

I was inside with the door shut behind me seconds later. Thin light came from somewhere ahead of me so I followed it, slowly and carefully, for the rest of the basement was pitch dark and I didn't want to stumble and knock over anything that might give me away.

My first thoughts were again of the crypt of the night before but the only smell down here was dry, coal dust, although it was hot, almost stiflingly so. I was glad reach the source of the light, which was a dim bulb hanging over a set of stone steps leading up into the main house.

This is where it got tricky.

I was chancing my luck even getting this far without notice. I stood inside the basement at a solid door that I knew would probably lead to the working parts of the house, somewhere near the kitchen that I already knew had a light on. So my chances of meeting somebody soon after opening that door were, at a guess, about fifty-fifty.

I've never been much of one for figuring the odds; if you need proof just ask Andy or Jock how much money they've taken off me at three-card brag over the years. As I said, I wasn't in the mood for over-thinking. I put a hand out, turned the handle and pushed the door open; if anyone had noticed, anyone said anything, I was prepared to reverse my way fast back out the cellar.

But my luck held enough for me to slip out into a quiet

corridor. I heard pans rattle and water run to my left where someone was working in the kitchen so I went right then quickly up the first flight of stairs I came to, hoping to avoid stumbling into whoever was doing his drinking in the room with the French windows.

And now I had a real problem; I had only thought as far as getting myself in. Now that I was there I hadn't a clue what I was going to do about it. I'd arrived with a vague idea of rescuing a girl but there was no Rapunzel here to let down her hair.

I took the simplest option available; I started trying doors, finding a variety of empty bedrooms in various states of decoration, a couple of recently modernised bathrooms and two old lavvies badly in need of a clean. What I didn't find was a girl.

I was starting to think that maybe Andy's connections were indeed, as Jock had put it, a load of pish, when I opened a door and the case opened up in front of me.

The woman in the room was sat in her night gown and robe at a dressing table and had her back to me but I saw her in the mirror clear enough and she saw me. Her eyes went wide, she looked ready to scream, so I stepped inside and put a hand over her mouth. While she was struggling in my arms I realised I knew her.

For being such a big city, Glasgow can sometimes be a small town and if you move in certain circles over a long period of time you end up meeting the same people at different points in their lives. At a previous point in this woman's life-- a woman who I guessed was the ex-Mrs Monaghan and current squeeze of the owner of this mansion—she'd been a teenager working a typewriter in a wee room at the bottom end of Maryhill Road in a pawnbroker's business.

"Jeanette," I said in her ear. "It's wee Jeanette fae Shettleston isn't it? Your daddie had an ice-cream van and your maw did hair. I remember you."

She went quiet at that, went still in my arms and didn't look ready to shout the house down so I gave here room to reply. She wasn't nearly as cultured as she'd been making herself look.

"Who the fuck are you and what the fuck are you doing here?"

"I'm the fuck looking for a wee lost lassie," I said. "Brunette, green duffel coat, presumed lost among your new man's wolves."

If she'd known about the girl I'd have expected a response but she showed no reaction except anger.

"I don't know what the fuck you're on about. Get out of my fucking house."

"That's a lot of fucks for a lady of the manor," I said. "Wee Pat Nolan would be proud of you."

That name finally got through to her. She went so limp I had to put her down on the bed, and se looked dazed when she looked up at me.

"Pat Nolan sent you? What's he got to do with this?"

"Pat? Nothing, he's been dead for years. But it's where I know you fae. You worked in Pat's office way back when. I was a pal of his."

She finally took the time to look me up and down properly.

"I ken you now. You got old."

"And you got rich. I think you're getting the better end of the deal. You're no' going to scream the house down are you?"

She shook her head.

"You're the most interesting thing that's happened in days. You got a fag?"

O ver the next half an hour and two of my smokes she found out I was on a job and I found out that she didn't have much of a clue what her man was up to. She'd graduated from Monaghan and saw almost anything after that as a step up; she wasn't asking too many questions of her new beau.

"He throws parties though?" I asked after a while, mostly to avoid noticing that her gown was slipping open. I was in a rich man's house, in his bedroom, with his scantily clad girlfriend. I didn't like my chances if he found me and got the cops involved.

"Aye, he has parties, in the auld ballroom downstairs. But it's men only, just his pals. He's got this wee club. Nae women invited, you ken what it's like? I'm no' even allowed into the room, he keeps it locked when they're no' using it."

"But he has lassies brought in, to keep his pals happy?"

She wasn't keen on answering that one and wouldn't meet my eye; it was obviously one of those questions she wasn't asking herself.

"You ken what men are like," she said after a time. "But the lassies are all fine afterwards. They get paid and sent back to town happy."

"That's what he tells you is it?"

She didn't answer that one either. So I told her what I'd found in the crypt in the Necropolis. I didn't know whether she believed that or not for before I could find out the man of the house walked into the room.

J oe Sullivan was a big man—in previous times he would have been called corpulent. His double chin hung over a bigger double chin and his belly strained mightily at the reinforced buttons of his expensive waistcoat. When he spoke it was in one of those faux-English upper class accents affected by Scots who've accumulated more money than sense.

"Mr. Adams, I presume? I was wondering when you were going to show up. Has Jeanette been showing you a good time?"

"Mostly she's been showing me that you're a piss-poor excuse for a boyfriend."

He laughed long and hard at that.

"At least I'm doing better than Monaghan. He got a bit hot under the collar, didn't he?"

Jeanette looked surprised at that.

"She doesn't know?" I asked.

"Know what?"

For once I was stumped. It wasn't my place to tell a woman her man, ex or not, had been burned to a crisp by something that came out of a mirror. I didn't even know where to start. Sullivan had no such qualms.

"He crossed me and got what was coming to him," he said to Jeanette. "Mr. Adams is looking to get much the same. But you don't need to worry about any of that, sweetheart. Have a drink. Have a few drinks. I'll be back up later."

I saw her think about replying then think about not. The latter won; I had a feeling it always won and she didn't say anything more as Sullivan motioned that I should follow him out of the room.

He put a hand on my arm. I replied in my best London

accent.

"You're a big man, but you're in bad shape. With me it's a full time job. Now behave yourself."

He laughed at that.

"I don't need muscle to deal with the likes of you," he said.

I pulled myself away from him, pushed him roughly to one side and headed for the stairs. His laughter followed me down the corridor.

I wondered why nobody gave chase.

I reached as far as the top of the staircase before I slowed. It wasn't voluntary, it was just that I suddenly hit a wall of treacle. Somebody laughed near my ear. It did, and didn't, sound like Sullivan. I know that doesn't make much sense but neither did the fact that I was straining to put one leg in front of another in what appeared to be nothing more than empty space.

It wasn't empty, I can tell you that for nowt. And it got warm, far warmer than even a summer's night had any right to be. I went down the stairs one painfully slow step at a time with sweat running down my brow and stinging my eyes. It felt like walking towards a furnace.

When I got to the bottom of the staircase, what seemed like an age later, every muscle straining, I tried to take a turn for the front door but whatever was slowing me down had other ideas. That strange doubled laugh echoed near my ear again as I was turned, a puppet in somebody else's hands, not for the front door but down the hallway towards the rear of the house to an old oak door that lay open showing flickering red shadows beyond.

The heat got more intense. The skin at my cheeks and brows tightened, my lips felt dry and cracked. I wondered whether it was possible for eyeballs to boil in their sockets and guessed I was going to find out pretty soon.

Then I was across the threshold and into the room beyond the oak door. I stumbled, almost fell as the pressure lifted off me and the heat fell away as if a fridge door had been opened somewhere. I stood in a high, vaulted ballroom of quite some opulence but at that moment all I had eyes for was the mirror above the fireplace at the far end from me. There was no fire set in the grate but the roaring flames inside the mirror were more than making up for that.

Sullivan spoke from behind me.

"Welcome to the latest incarnation of the Hellfire Club, Mr. Adams, although I believe your membership will be, of necessity, a short one."

Sullivan motioned that I should move through the room. My legs decided they were going to obey him.

The room was the kind of place where they used to film *The White Heather Club* back in the day. If you're old enough to remember that you're old enough to know what I'm talking about. The rest of you can just imagine *Four Weddings and a Funeral.* In Scotland. It was all old paneling, shields on the wall, marquetry flooring and twinkling chandeliers. The flickering red from the mirror made it look like a dancing vision of what might be my personal hell.

"Sit," he said, forcibly as if addressing a recalcitrant dog.

I went over and sat, without any conscious effort on my own part, in what was thankfully a comfortable armchair some twelve feet away from the fireplace, facing the damned mirror. When I tried to rise again I found that I could move everything from my waist up, but the lower part of me seemed to have turned to cold stone and my arse felt like it had been super-glued to the seat.

"You will stay there until we are ready to have you move," Sullivan said in the same commanding tone and I knew I would be obeying; the choice in the matter wasn't mine.

"Can I at least smoke?"

"You can burst into flames for all I care," Sullivan replied and his loud laugh echoed around the ballroom, the strange double effect kicking in on its second pass around.

My fingers trembled as I got a smoke lit but I managed to keep it out of my voice.

"Okay, you got me. So what now?"

"I told you. You're an honorary member of the Club. I need to call a special meeting for tomorrow night so you'll have to stay where you are until then but I can assure you, you are going to see one hell of a show. Not only that, you'll be the star turn."

And with that he left me. I heard a key turn in a heavy lock then silence fell. The sole source of light in the room came from the flames in the mirror but there was no heat in them.

A car went off down the driveway, rattling the gravel; the kitchen help going home after their shift. A door shut upstairs somewhere; Sullivan making for his queen's bedchamber. After that quiet fell in the house.

I don't believe I have ever felt so alone.

It took me ten minutes to remember I had a phone in my pocket; that shows you how spooked I was. But it wasn't going to be any help to me; when I switched it on the screen showed only red, flickering, flames dancing in time with the ones in the mirror.

I tried shouting for a while but after a few minutes it

began to tear at my throat and it was obvious that even if someone heard nobody gave a fuck.

Using my hands I pushed down on the arms of the chair, hoping to at least be able to lever myself off onto the floor and crawl away if I had to but all I did was ache and pull a muscle at my left shoulder. After that I did some more shouting despite my ragged throat.

Still no one came.

At some point later I started in on the half bottle of whisky that I still had in my inside pocket. What with that, the fags and the three, partially melted, bars of chocolate, I was going to survive the night but I wasn't at all sure that I wanted to.

The laughter began somewhere around midnight.

At first I thought it was mice, a rustling whisper just at the limit of hearing, but it quickly grew to a soft liquid chuckle, a deep bass tone that I was unable to make myself believe came from Sullivan. The sound echoed around me such that I couldn't pinpoint its source. First it came from somewhere around the main chandelier but as it got louder it was somewhere near the mirror of flames then, worse than that, only feet behind me, a whispering laugh in my ear. If it had been regular I might have fallen in to being able to ignore it as background noise, but sometimes there were long minutes between occurrences, other times the laughing came every few seconds.

It was slowly driving me mad and no amount of smokes or chocolate would settle me. I gave in to the urge and made a headlong dive into the whisky, necking it down as fast as it would come out of the bottle.

Something laughed heartily as blessed oblivion finally took me away into darkness.

I came out of it to watery morning sunlight coming in from a window almost at my back and someone shouting my name from that direction. I tried to turn to see but my head doesn't go all the way round, more so when I have a hangover. The voice was a woman's though and I only knew one woman here.

"Jeanette?" I shouted. "Get me the fuck out of here. This is no fucking kind of party at all."

I don't know if she heard me, but she stopped shouting. Shadows moved as if someone had stepped away from the window then I was alone, just my hangover for company. At least the laughter had stopped but after a while I might even have welcomed that; the whisky was gone, the chocolate was only a sweet memory and I was getting through my supply of smokes too fast.

Nobody came over the course of a long morning and longer afternoon. Thankfully I hadn't drank enough fluids to need to pish but that got me wondering, for I couldn't feel much of anything below the waist. For all I knew I might have pished, or even shat, myself in the night. My sense of smell was intact though and that could only smell whisky and smoke so I guessed I was okay for a while yet. But the longer it went with no one coming, the more I knew that a wee accident might well be forthcoming.

And all the time those godawful flames kept flickering away in the mirror, a fire that no one—no one on this side of it anyway—ever needed to stoke.

I spent my time wondering; whether it had been Jeanette at the window, whether George had got my voicemail of the night before and what he might do with the info the longer it went with no word from me. But mainly I wondered what

Sullivan had in store for me in the night to come. The flickering flames served as a constant reminder of my worst fear. I resolved I would do everything in my power to avoid going the same way as Monaghan, no matter what it took.

Finally, and only when the sun had moved round and shadows started to creep in the corners of the ballroom, I heard the sound of a key in the heavy lock.

"Jeanette?" I said hopefully, but got Sullivan's laugh in reply.

"You should be so lucky," he said. "But you've got no feeling below the waist. What use would she be to you?" He came in wheeling a drink's cabinet in front of him and rolled it up to beside the fire. "Won't be long now. I couldn't quite get everybody on such short notice but most of the club should be here in an hour so. We'll have a few drinks, something to eat, then we'll get the party started proper."

"Don't go out of your way on my behalf," I said with more bravery than I felt at that moment.

"Oh, this isn't for you," he replied. "This is for us. Tonight will be a rededication of our vows, for all of us. He calls for it, from time to time."

I didn't bother asking who Sullivan was referring to; I had a good idea by then.

He came over and took the whisky bottle and chocolate wrappers out of my lap and cleaned up the ash and cigarette ends I'd been letting fall to the floor. He moved primly, fastidiously, lips pursed all the time as if I'd offended his sensibilities. Right then I wished I had shat myself, if only to offend him further.

As he bent close to me I made a grab for him but my fingers only touched his hair and he stepped nimbly away before I could try to get a punch in.

"Still some fight in you yet then? That's good. He likes a bit of fight. He revels in it."

And with that I was left alone again with the growing darkness and my smokes. A succession of cars came up the drive, roaring on the gravel, and doors opened and shut round the house. My stomach growled in reply as I smelled cooking and a wee bit later I heard the distant clatter of cutlery and plates with accompanying voices raised in conversation. There was a dining room somewhere close where guests were being wined and dined. I was the beggar at the feast; worse off than even that, for no one came to throw me some scraps.

A nd now we come to it.

It was getting on for dark again before they came and I was hearing the mouse-whisperer high near the chandelier so I was actually glad of the company.

I can't say that I was surprised to recognize some of the club's patrons. Several of them I knew from the photies in the paperwork I'd been sent, faces with no names. But there were others that I knew from the papers and TV news, and even two guys who I'd class as passing acquaintances, one of whom I'd even done a favor for some years passed. He in particular refused to look me in the eye.

"Hi, John," I said loudly. "Remember when I found that necklace your missus lost? Get me out of this fucking chair and we'll call it evens."

He went to the drink's cabinet and pointedly kept his back to me. They all got their glasses stocked, then the party began.

It was boring as hell; too much drink and none of it for me for one thing. At some point Sullivan had a telly and a DVD player wheeled in and they all watched some pretty tame porn. Some of them had a furtive wank, others shouted cheerfully at the antics on screen and the whole thing reminded me of student beer nights in the University Union. I'd been bloody bored then too.

"You call this Hellfire?" I said after a while. "When do you start enjoying yourself?"

"I wouldn't have thought you'd be in such a hurry to get to the end of the night, Mr. Adams," Sullivan said. His face was near as red as the flickering flames, his lips moist and ugly. "But if you insist. I've got a wee surprise for you first though, something you get to see before it's your turn."

That's when they brought the lassie in.

They had her drugged up with something; her mouth and eyes had yon tell tale slack look and Sullivan had to herd her in from the doorway to stand her in front of the mirror. She wore only a thin, gauze-like gown through which you could see everything you shouldn't be seeing.

I'd have liked her better in her green duffel coat.

T he men in the room were all stood in a semicircle, all eyes on the girl.

"You sick fuckers," I said to Sullivan.

"I like to think so," he replied as if taking a compliment then I went quiet, for the heat had risen noticeably with the lass's entry and I'd started to sweat again.

Sullivan stood beside the girl in front of the mirror, raised both hands and intoned seriously.

In nomine magni dei nostri Satanas, introibo ad altare Domini Inferi

The flames quickened and the heat rose to wash over us as if a furnace had been opened.

"We are gathered to pledge our allegiance, master," Sullivan said, a sing-song voice, almost a chant. "We thank you for your munificence. Accept this, our humble sacrifice."

At that the tattoo on my arm throbbed and suddenly I wasn't thinking about the flames; I was thinking about wee Pat Nolan's pawnshop, his teenage secretary, sigils, totems, a house in Hyndland Road, two lost lasses and mirror magic. I was thinking about coincidences and how I don't believe in them.

The flames roared higher in the mirror and the bass, chuckling of laughter rolled through the ballroom. The heat rose and rose again. Below the mirror a fire roared into life in the empty grate and Sullivan laughed as loudly as his master.

As for me, I was trying to shut everything out, lost and away several years in the past with a different lass, Alex Seton, and a different mirror, one that she'd negated with her magic. As I said, I don't believe in coincidences; somebody, somewhere was trying to tell me something.

I was trying to listen.

As they had in Monaghan's conservatory the flames rushed forward from deep in the mirror to the front. A finger of fire slid out from inside the glass and dropped, dripping, to the hearth. It came towards the drugged lassie, a wee river of flame heading for her toes.

The thing I'd been trying to remember finally came to me; I didn't recollect it so much as hear it in Alex Seton's voice in my head and all I had to do was chant along with her, her Gaelic against Sullivan's Latin. I knew which side my money was on.

"Ri linn tabhar na breithe Biodh a shith air do theannal fein.
"Dhumna Ort!"

The effect was immediate. The stone that held me to the chair fell away and I launched myself out of it. My legs cramped immediately from having been stuck in the same place for the best part of twenty four hours but even that helped my cause for it kept me low and I went straight for my target as if throwing myself into a rugby scrum.

My head caught Sullivan just below his belly and my weight toppled him backward to the floor.

The finger of fire found his hair and began to eat as the bass laughter echoed louder and louder around us.

Things get a wee bit hazy for the next few minutes.

For a start, a brick came through the window, a woman's voice shouted, "I hope you burn in hell, you fucker," and George from the Two Dugs came into the room with six guys who looked like they'd be joining me in a scrum.

Sullivan screamed, his feet thrashed at the hardwood floor. The flame found his mouth, poured into him and the rest went much the same way as it had with Monaghan, although Sullivan burned for longer and hotter; he was a big man, and carried a lot of fat.

The other members of the Hellfire Club scarpered fast; whether George let them go for the sake of his business interests I'll never know and at that point I didn't really care. By this time I had the wee lassie in my arms and I wasn't going to let her out of my sight until I got her to her grannie.

George handed me a tall glass filled with expensive whisky and I let it do its job while we watched a fucker burn.

That's about it.

The wee lassie was reunited with her grannie the next

morning; I left them together before the waterworks flooded me out. Old Joe was as good as his word, paid my expenses and wrote off my smokes tab, even gave me two extra packs in thanks.

Over a pint the next lunchtime Jock and Andy got a new story to add to their repertoire.

I phoned Liz, told her where to find what was left of Sullivan and gave her the names that I knew of the rest of the infernal club; it's up to her now whether she does anything with that info.

Wee Jeanette? I found out later that it had been her that effected the rescue; after failing to get my attention at the window in the morning, she'd phoned round old associates of Pat Nolan and finally made her way to George, who called up the cavalry.

The big house was burning, mirror and all when George and I left it; George had brought three transit vans with him and he'd filled them with some good stuff from the furnishing and fittings, so he did okay out of it in the end.

We left the mirror where it was though.

There's one other wee thing.

As I turned to leave the ballroom for the last time, I had a final look in the mirror. There were no flames now, just my reflection in the doorway. But just for a second it was as if somebody was standing beside me, somebody that took my hand and kissed me gently on the cheek.

I might, or might not have felt it.

It matters, either way.

ABOUT THE MIDNIGHT EYE

I read widely, both in the crime and horror genres, but my crime fiction in particular keeps returning to older, pulpier, bases.

My series character, Glasgow PI Derek Adams, is a Bogart and Chandler fan, and it is the movies and Americana of the '40s that I find a lot of my inspiration for him, rather than in the modern procedural.

That, and the old city, are the two main drivers for the Midnight Eye stories.

When I was a lad, back in the early 1960s, we lived in a town 20 miles south of Glasgow, and it was an adventure to the big city when I went with my family on shopping trips. Back then the city was a Victorian giant going slowly to seed.

It is often said that the British Empire was built in Glasgow on the banks of the river Clyde. Back when I was young, the shipyards were still going strong, and the city centre itself still held on to some of its past glories.

It was a warren of tall sandstone buildings and narrow streets, with Edwardian trams still running through them. The big stores still had pneumatic delivery systems for billing, every man wore a hat, collar and tie, and steam trains ran into grand vaulted railway stations filled with smoke.

By the time I was a student in the late '70s, a lot of the tall sandstone buildings had been pulled down to make way for tower blocks. Back then they were the new shiny future, taking the people out of the Victorian ghettos and into the present day.

Fast forward to the present day and there are all new ghettos. The tower blocks are ruled by drug gangs and pimps. Meanwhile there have been many attempts to gentrify the city centre, with designer shops being built in old warehouses, with docklands developments building expensive apartments where sailors used to get services from hard faced girls, and with shiny, trendy bars full of glossy expensively dressed bankers.

And underneath it all the old Glasgow still lies, slumbering, a dreaming god waiting for the stars to be right again. It can be found in the places where Derek walks, in bars untouched by time, in the closes of tenement buildings that carry the memories of past glories, and in the voices of older men and women who travel through the modernity unseen, impervious to its charms.

Derek Adams, The Midnight Eye, knows the ways of the old city. And, if truth be told, he prefers them to the new.

There are antecedents - occult detectives who may seem to use the trappings of crime solvers, but get involved in the supernatural. William Hjortsberg's Falling Angel (the book that led to the movie Angel Heart) is a fine example, an expert blending of gumshoe and deviltry that is one of my favorite books. Likewise, in the movies, we have cops facing a demon in Denzel Washington's Fallen that plays like a police procedural taken to a very dark place.

But I think it's the people that influence me most. Everybody in Scotland's got stories to tell, and once you get them going, you can't stop them. I love chatting to people, (usually in pubs) and finding out the -weird- stuff they've experienced. Derek is mainly based on a bloke I met years ago in a bar in Partick, and quite a few of the characters that turn up and talk too much in my books can be found in real life in bars in Glasgow, Edinburgh and St Andrews.

Derek has been with me from very close to the start of my writing career; the first short story, THE JOHNSON AMULET that later turned into the first novel, was among the earliest things I wrote back in late 1992. He's turned up in three novels so far, THE AMULET, THE SIRENS and THE SKIN GAME, all still available singly in ebook at all the usual online stores, in print in THE MIDNIGHT EYE OMNIBUS Volume 1 and in individual shiny audiobook editions, all available from Gryphonwood Press.

THE AMULET is also out in a Portuguese language edition from Retropunk Publicadoes in Brazil and there's a German language edition of THE AMULET from Blitz Verlag.

There are a handful of Midnight Eye short stories collected in the omnibus editions, in the second of which they are alongside three novellas; RHYTHM AND BOOZE (also in my Dark Melodies collection), DEAL OR NO DEAL (also available as a free sampler in ebook from Gryphonwood

Press), and FARSIDE (also in the OCCULT DETECTIVE QUARTERLY PRESENTS anthology from Ulthar Press.)

GREEN DOOR represented the start of the next stage of work for Derek and is his introduction to my Sigils and Totems mythos.

Derek has developed a life of his own, and I'm along for the ride.

ABOUT ME

I am a Scottish writer, now living in Canada, with over thirty novels published in the genre press and over 300 short story credits in thirteen countries.

I have books available from a variety of publishers including Dark Regions Press and Severed Press, and my work has appeared in a number of professional anthologies and magazines with recent sales to NATURE Futures, Penumbra and Buzzy Mag among others.

I live in Newfoundland with whales, bald eagles and icebergs for company and when I'm not writing I drink beer, play guitar and dream of fortune and glory.

Willie
williammeikle.com

OTHER BOOKS BY WILLIAM MEIKLE

NOVELS

The S-Squad Series
Berserker
Crustaceans
Eldren: The Book of the Dark
Fungoid
Generations
Island Life
Night of the Wendigo
Ramskull
Sherlock Holmes: The Dreaming Man
Songs of Dreaming Gods
The Boathouse
The Creeping Kelp
The Dunfield Terror
The Exiled
The Green and the Black
The Hole
The Invasion
The Midnight Eye Files: The Amulet
The Midnight Eye Files: The Sirens
The Midnight Eye Files: The Skin Game
The Ravine
The Valley
The Concordances of the Red Serpent
Watchers: The Battle for the Throne
Watchers: The Coming of the King
Watchers: Culloden
The Road Hole Bunker Mystery
Hound of Night / Veil Knights #2 (as Rowan Casey)

NOVELLAS

Broken Sigil
Clockwork Dolls
Pentacle
Professor Challenger: The Island of Terror
Sherlock Holmes: Revenant
The House on the Moor
The Job
The Midnight Eye Files: Deal or No Deal
The Plasm
The CopyCat Murders
Tormentor

SHORT STORY COLLECTIONS

Carnacki: Heaven and Hell
Carnacki: The Edinburgh Townhouse
Carnacki: The Watcher at the Gate
Dark Melodies
Myth and Monsters
Professor Challenger: The Kew Growths
Samurai and Other Stories
Sherlock Holmes: The Quality of Mercy
The Ghost Club
Home From the Sea
Into The Black
Flower of Scotland
Augustus Seton: Collected Chronicles
Bug Eyed Monsters

Details of all of these works and more can be found at his website at
williammeikle.com

Printed in Great Britain
by Amazon